This Walker book belongs to:

_____

_____

_____

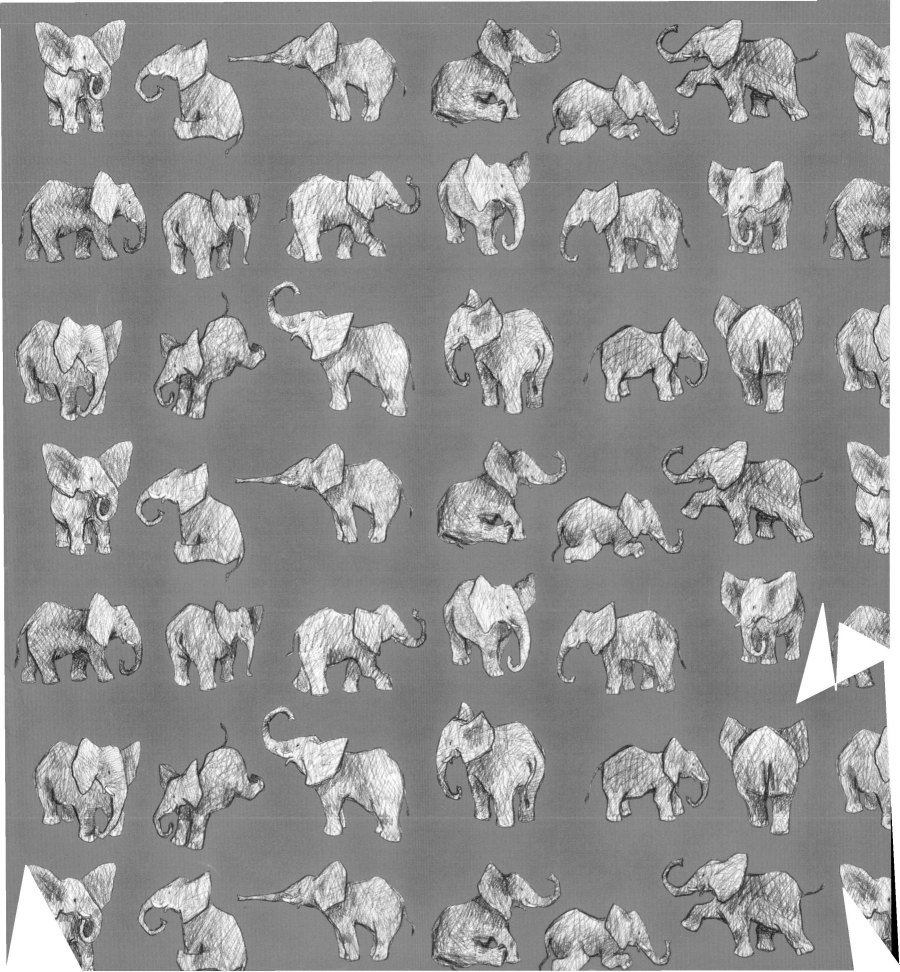

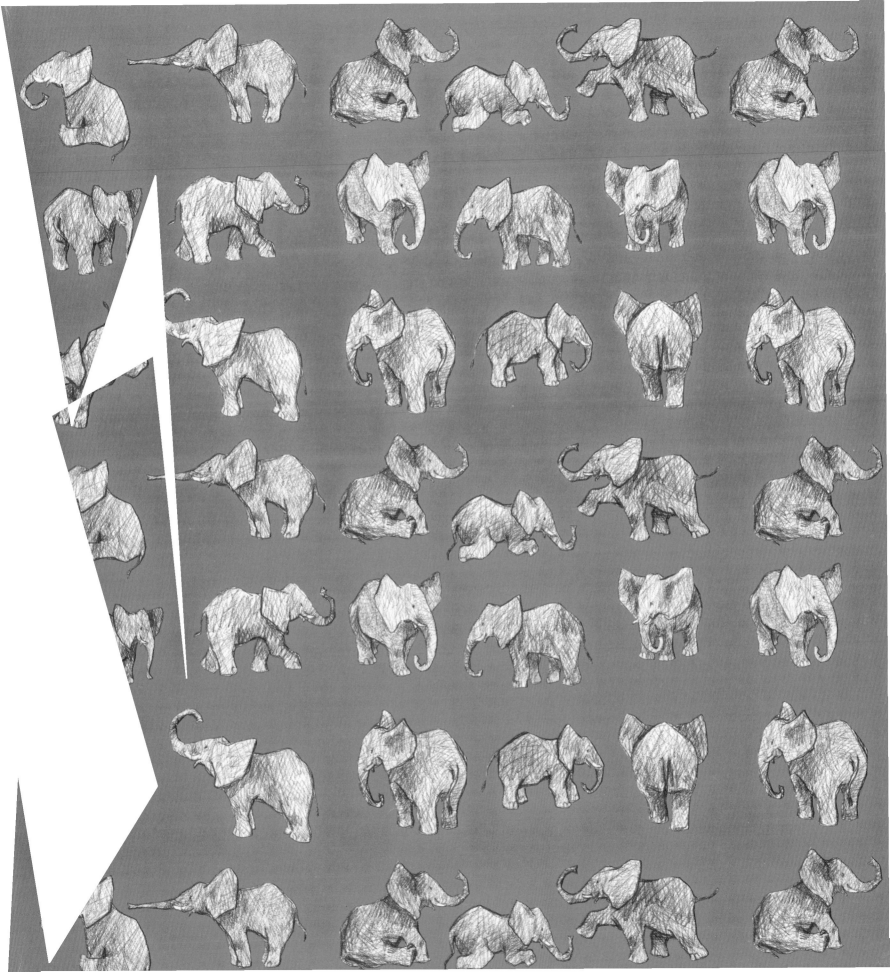

To Marin, Vincent and Max

E L E P

Petr Horáček

HA _ _ T

WALKER BOOKS
AND SUBSIDIARIES
LONDON • BOSTON • SYDNEY • AUCKLAND

I asked Grandad to play football with me, but he was too busy.

I went to
see Grandma
but she was
busy too.

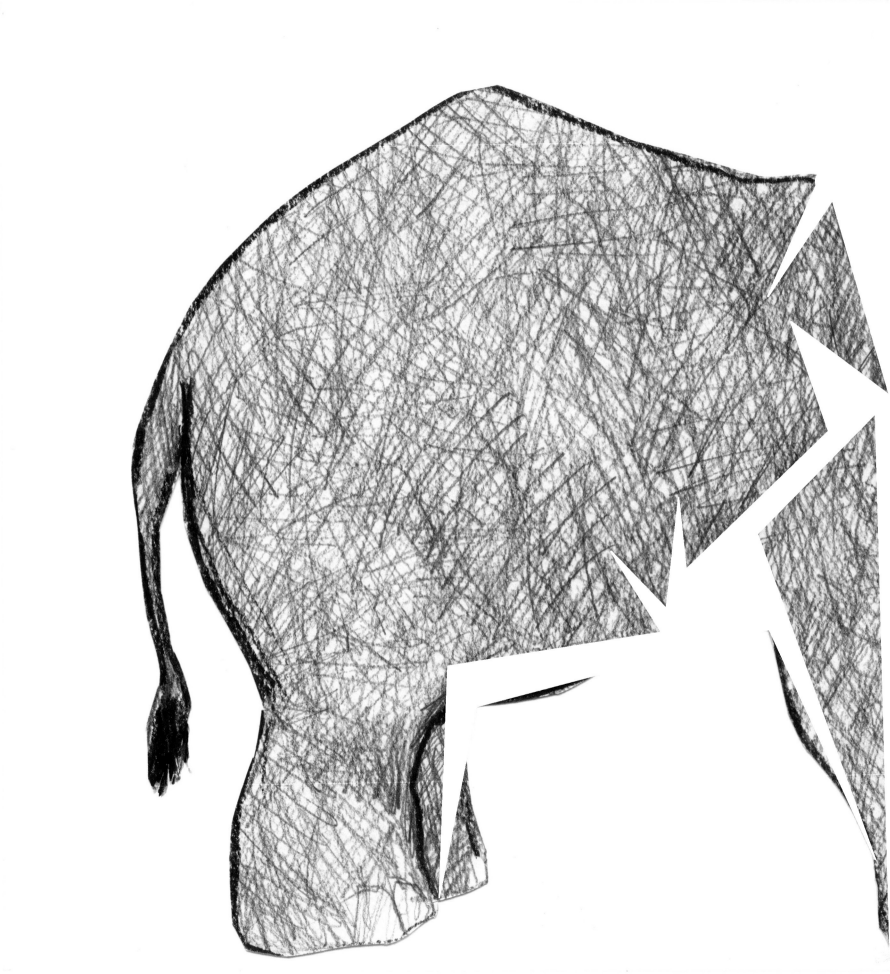

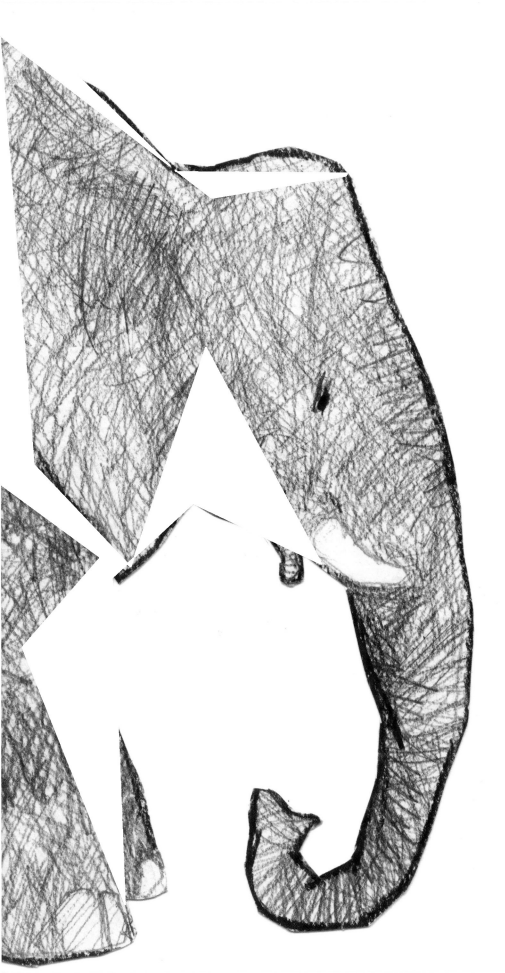

So I
asked my
ELEPHANT
if HE
wanted
to play
with me.

We played football
in the garden.

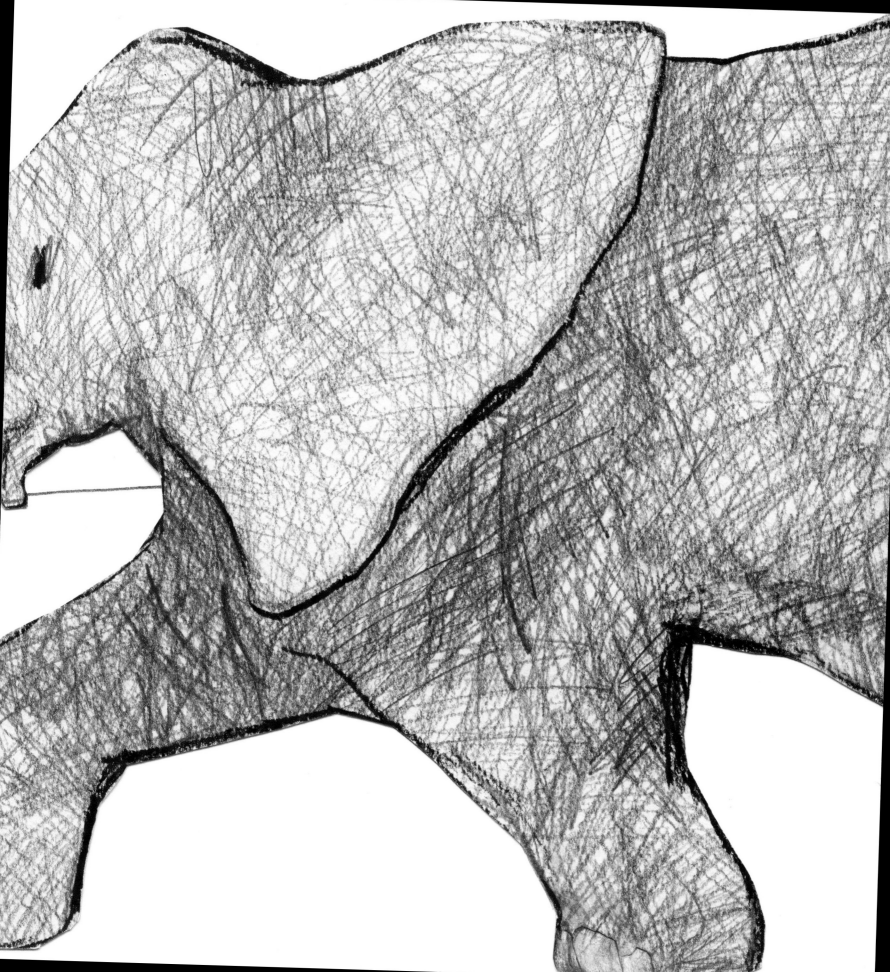

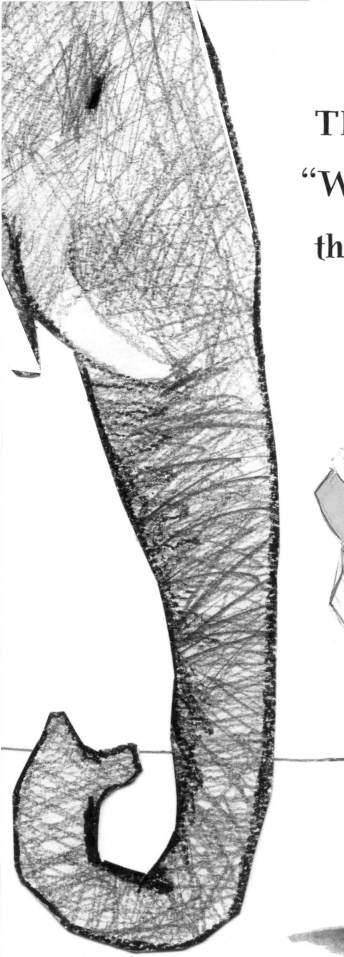

Then Grandad called,
"Who MESSED UP
the flowerbed?"

"I'm sorry,
it was my
ELEPHANT,"
I replied.

Grandad did not believe me,
so I took my ELEPHANT inside.

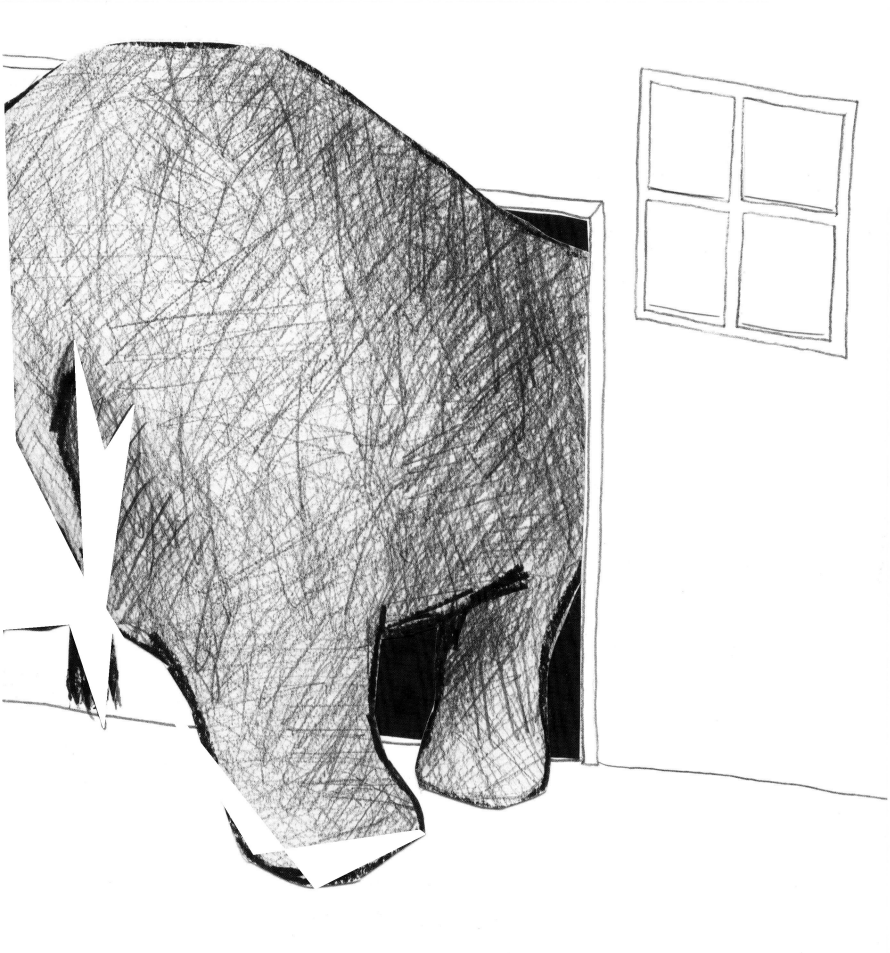

Then Grandma called,
"Who MESSED UP the hallway?"

"I'm sorry, but it must have
been my ELEPHANT,"
I replied.

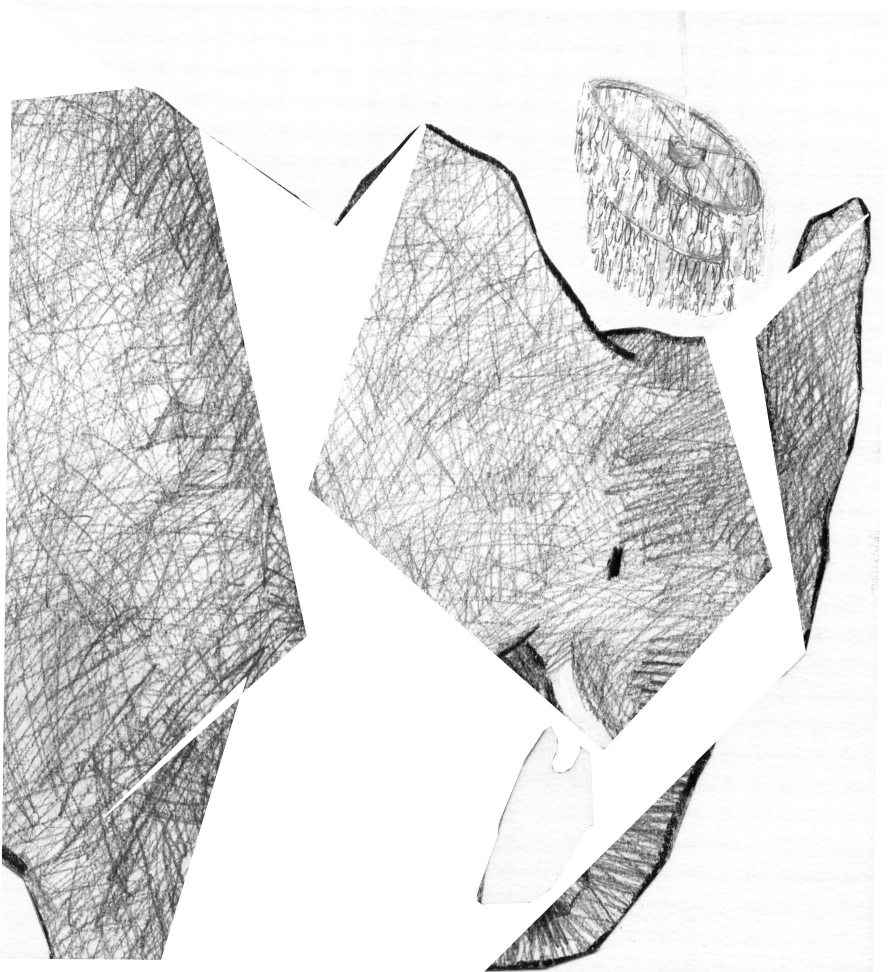

"And was it your
ELEPHANT
who

SPLASHED

and

made

puddles

in the

bathroom?"

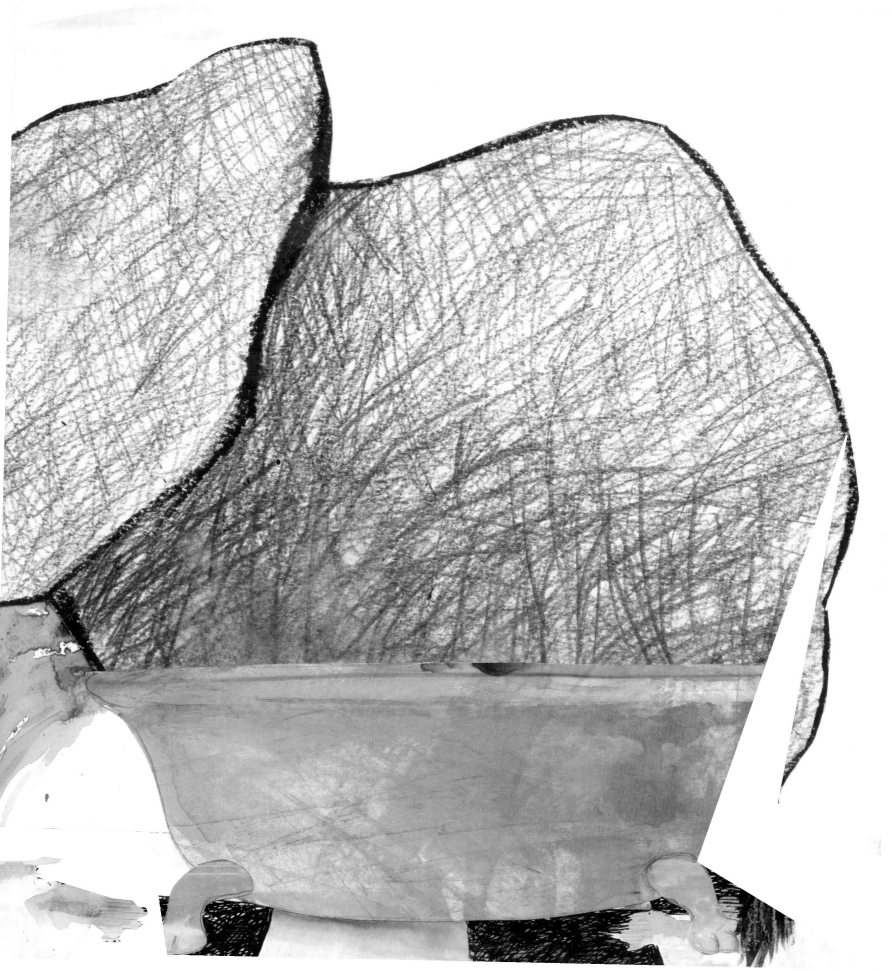

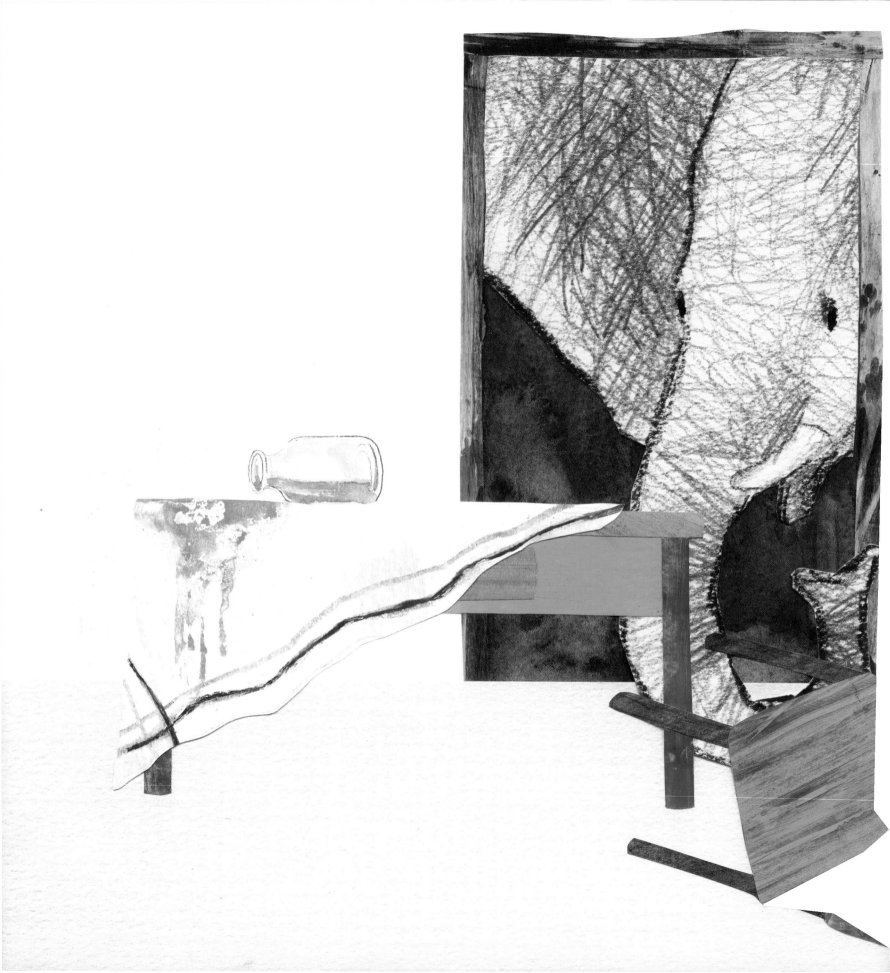

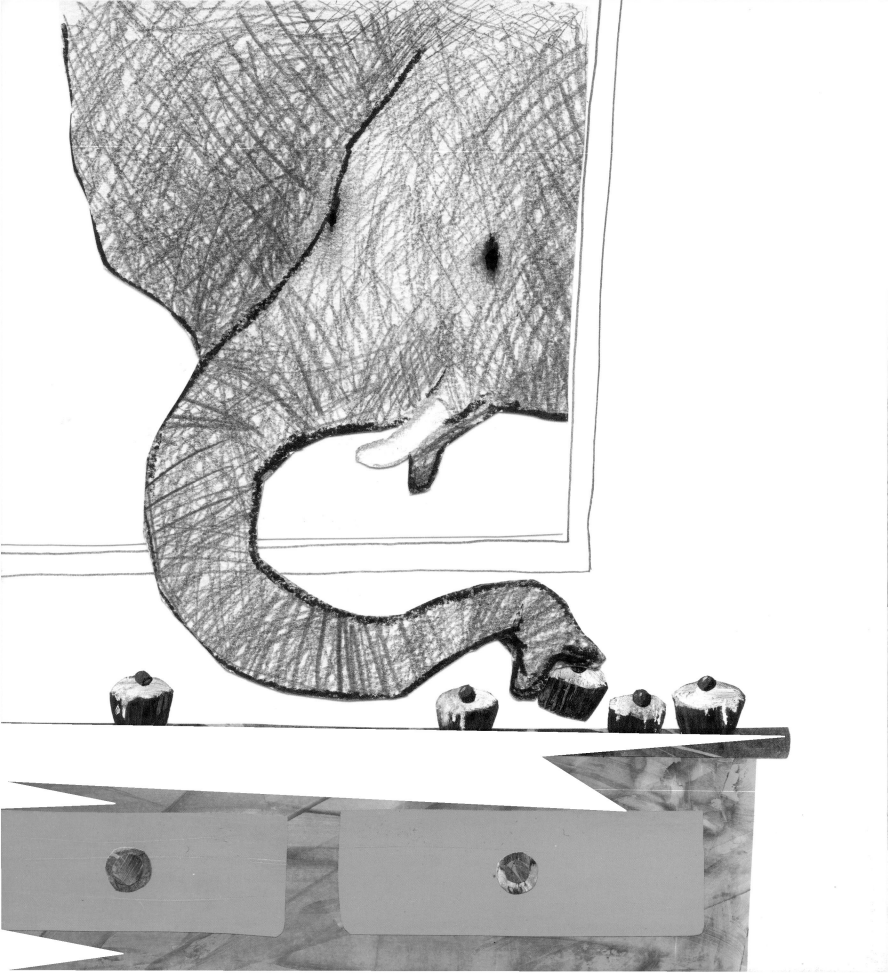

"And was it your ELEPHANT who ATE some of the cakes?" Grandma asked.

"Well ... yes," I replied truthfully. Grandma looked at me as if she didn't believe me.

I was upset.

I wanted

to be

alone.

Then my ELEPHANT
came. He smiled at
me. I said sorry
for telling
on him.

We were
friends
again.

We played in my room all day.

We went fishing. It was fun.

Then my ELEPHANT took me to
the jungle to see tigers until ...

it was
morning
and
Grandad
wanted
to play
football.

"But how did I get
to bed?" I asked.

"You were tired…"
said Grandad.

"So your ELEPHANT took you to bed!"

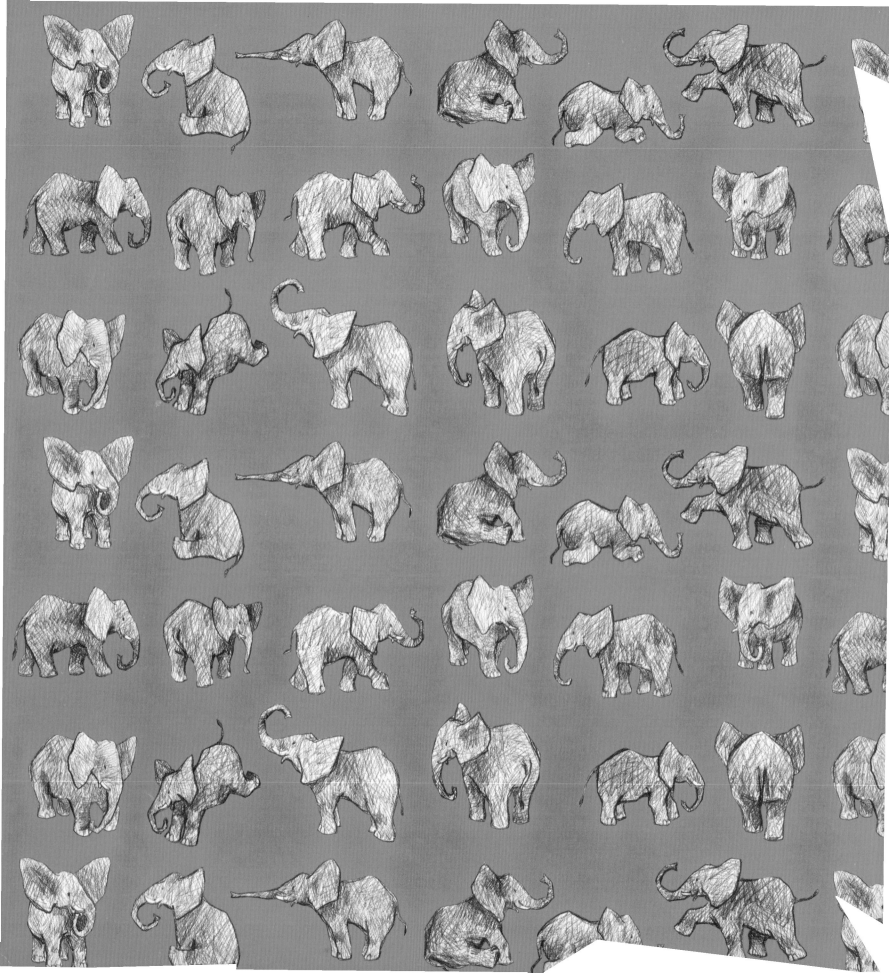

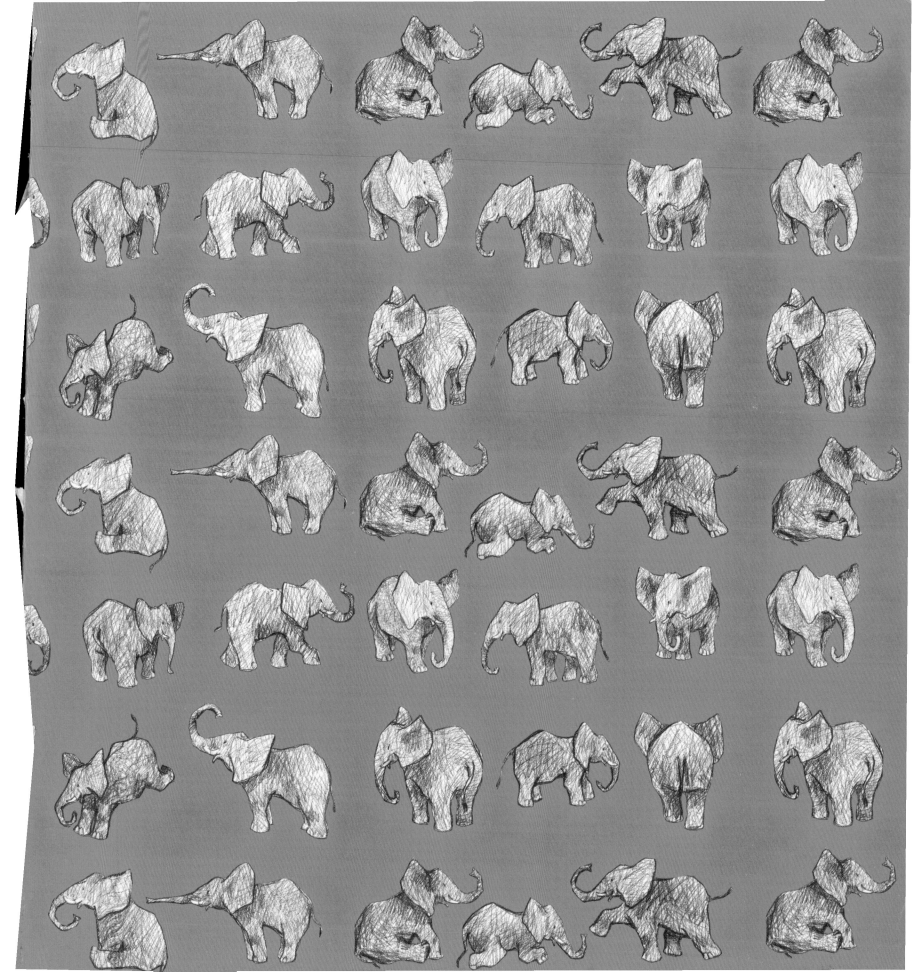

Other books by Petr Horáček

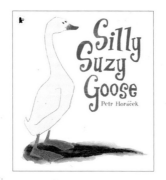

Silly Suzy Goose
ISBN 978-1-4063-0458-9

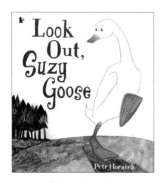

Look Out, Suzy Goose
ISBN 978-1-4063-1764-0

Suzy Goose and the Christmas Star
ISBN 978-1-4063-2065-7

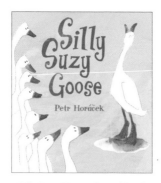

Silly Suzy Goose Board Book
ISBN 978-1-4063-1876-0

Beep Beep
ISBN 978-1-4063-2505-8

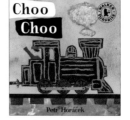

Choo Choo
ISBN 978-1-4063-2506-5

Butterfly Butterfly
ISBN 978-1-84428-844-1

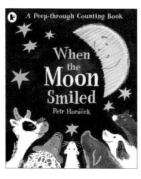

When the Moon Smiled
ISBN 978-0-7445-7047-2

A New House for Mouse
ISBN 978-1-4063-0122-9

This Little Cat
ISBN 978-1-4063-2511-9

Hello, Little Bird
ISBN 978-1-4063-2508-9

Run, Mouse, Run!
ISBN 978-1-4063-2509-6

Flutter by, Butterfly
ISBN 978-1-4063-2507-2

Strawberries are Red
ISBN 978-1-4063-2510-2

What is Black and White?
ISBN 978-1-4063-2512-6

Available from all good bookstores

www.walker.co.uk